Kathleen Pennell

MISSING MONEY

by Kathleen Pennell

illustrated by
Lauren Pennell

MISSING MONEY
PONY INVESTIGATORS #1

Library of Congress Number: 00-135993
International Standard Book Number: 1-930353-21-9

Printed 2000 by
Masthof Press
219 Mill Road
Morgantown, PA 19543-9701

Dedicated

to

Greg, Steve and Denise, and Lauren

Many thanks also to:

Miss Courtney Noonan

student at Lancaster Country Day School

Mrs. Deborah Noonan

school librarian, East York School District

Miss Chelsey Turner

fellow boarder at Hammer Creek Farm

Contents

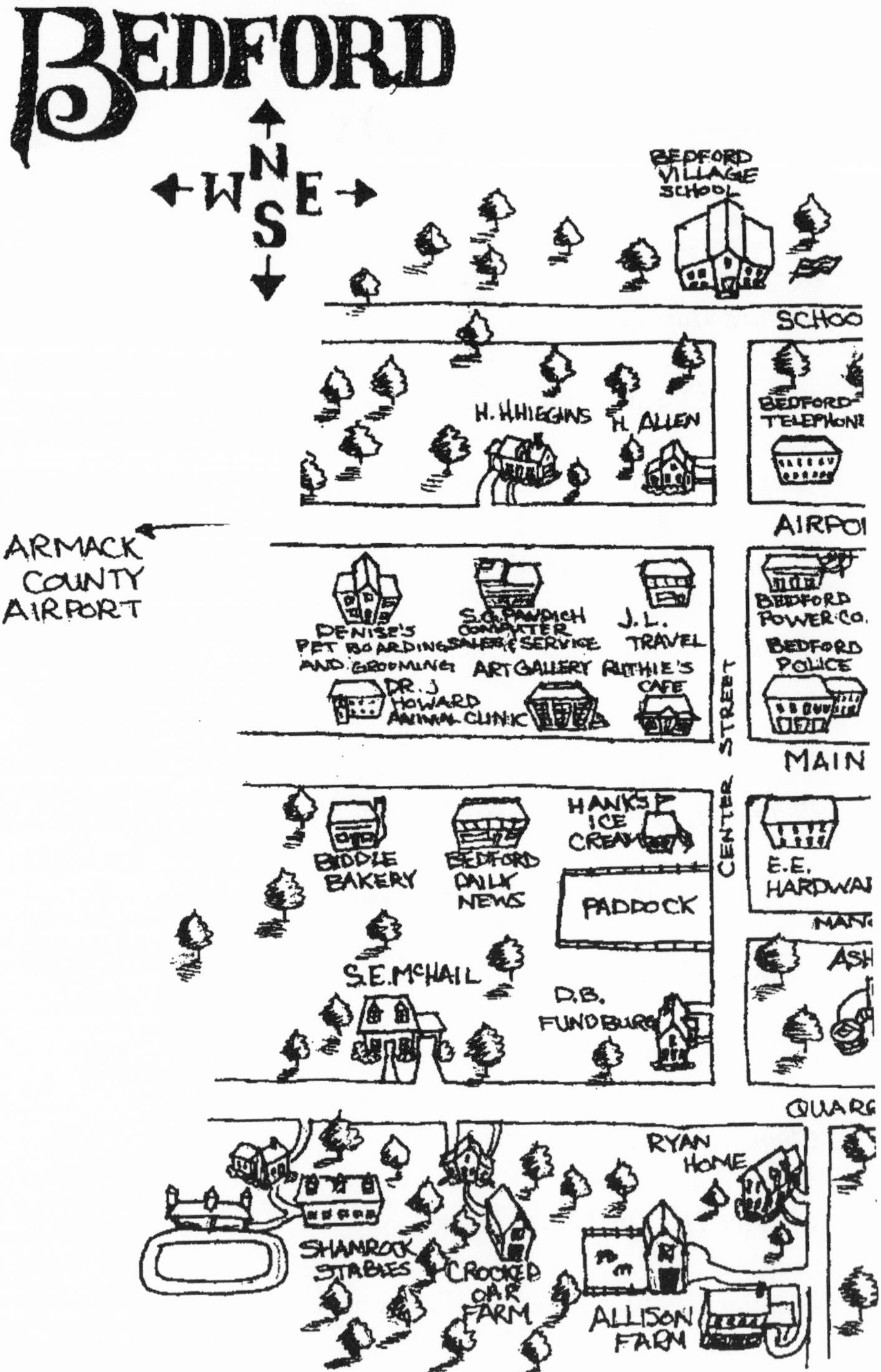

BEDFORD
N
W
E
S
BEDFORD VILLAGE SCHOOL
SCHOO
H. HHIGGINS
H. ALLEN
BEDFORD TELEPHON
AIRPO
ARMACK COUNTY AIRPORT
DENISE'S PET BOARDING AND GROOMING
J.L. TRAVEL
BEDFORD POWER CO.
BEDFORD POLICE
ART GALLERY
RUTHIE'S CAFE
DR. J HOWARD ANIMAL CLINIC
CENTER STREET
MAIN
HANK'S ICE CREAM
BIDDLE BAKERY
BEDFORD DAILY NEWS
PADDOCK
E.E. HARDWA
MAN
ASH
S.E. McHAIL
D.B. FUNDBURG
QUAR
RYAN HOME
SHAMROCK STABLES
CROOKED OAK FARM
ALLISON FARM

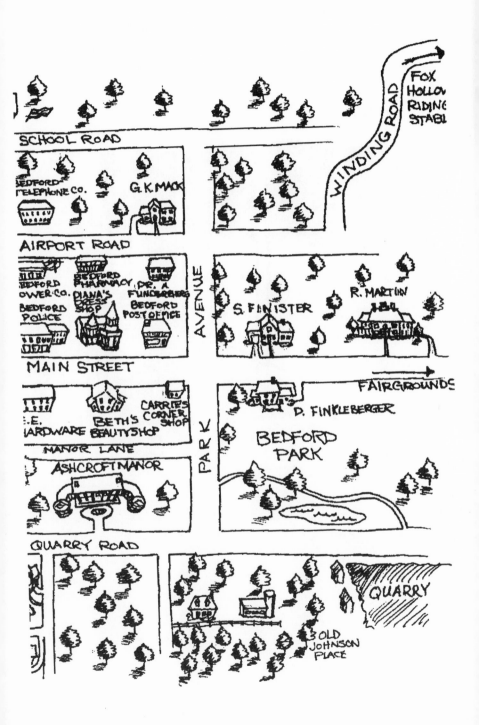

CHAPTER 1

Time's Running Out

Amy Jo leveled the sharp end of the pitchfork right above his belt. "Get back!" she shouted, her hands trembling.

The man's dark eyes narrowed as he advanced, slowly twisting the lead line with one hand, snapping the clasp open and shut with the other.

It was his hands that terrified her. They were shaped like claws.

"Time's running out," he continued, menacingly. "They'll be here tomorrow." His voice seemed to echo down the aisle of the barn.

Backing up a step Amy Jo looked over her shoulder. "A few more days, that's all I need," she pleaded, her entire body shaking now. "Can't you just give me a little more time?"

His brown rumpled suit pressed against the pitchfork as he said accusingly. "It's your fault, Amy Jo, your fault, Amy Jo, Amy Jo—"

*　　　*　　　*　　　*

It was her mother leaning over her.

Amy Jo sat up blinking her eyes.

1

"You've got to stop reading those mystery stories right before you fall asleep," said Elizabeth Ryan, tiredly sitting down on the edge of her daughter's bed.

"It must have been the pickles I ate with the pepperoni pizza last night," she decided, rubbing her stomach.

Mrs. Ryan pushed back her auburn hair. "What were you dreaming?" she asked, crossing her arms and cupping her chin in her right hand.

Amy Jo took a deep breath. "Mr. Alltauk was in it." She gave her mother a knowing look.

"Hm, the real estate man," she said, closing her eyes.

Amy Jo nodded. "The new people are supposed to move into the house back the lane tomorrow," she continued, "and I haven't been able to find a new home for the ponies. He's been calling me every day." She sighed and leaned back in bed. "He threatened to take them to the glue factory."

Mrs. Ryan's eyes flew open. "He what!?"

"I mean in my dream."

"Oh," said Mrs. Ryan, closing her eyes again. "Is there a chance the new family will let them stay?"

Amy Jo shrugged her shoulders. "I asked him about it last night, but he won't even talk to the new people about it. There's supposed to be a girl. She might even *like* ponies, but I think the parents bought the farm without her even seeing it."

Mrs. Ryan leaned over and kissed her daughter on the forehead. "It'll all work out, dear," she said, patting her arm as she got up to leave.

2

"I'll stick around the barn tomorrow until they'll show up," said Amy Jo sleepily as she rolled over. "I'll think of something."

*   *   *   *

"Glue factory," muttered Amy Jo disgustedly, fingering the nose of her chestnut pony, Ginger. "Over my dead body," she said as she peeked between the slats into the next stall at Oreo. Shaking her head she walked across the aisle to get the pitchfork and muck bucket.

Tossing the muck bucket into the corner of Ginger's stall, she stabbed at the dirty straw as if it were the enemy.

Moments later, Amy Jo cocked her head at the sound of a car pulling over the gravel. Her eyes narrowed as she latched the stall door and made her way down the aisle. Edging the barn door open, she peered outside. It was her nightmare from last night pacing back and forth in his rumpled brown suit, looking at his watch. She took a firmer grip on her pitchfork as her eyes traveled down the length of his coat to his smooth hands, then shook the memory of claws from last night's dream.

The ponies neighed softly. "I'm thinking, I'm thinking," she said guiltily, chewing on her lip.

More crunching gravel. Her heart sank as another car rounded the curve.

Amy Jo stared into space for a moment, then her eyes became thoughtful as she drew the door silently closed. "Maybe it'll work," she murmured hopefully.

A broad-shouldered man eased himself stiffly out of the car, then reached behind and opened the back door.

"Come on, Becky," he said, stretching his tall frame.

A girl slid out, pulled a scrunchy from her jeans pocket, and drew her dark hair back into a ponytail. Her hazel eyes studied the two-story house to her right. It was white and had black shutters with a connecting shed at the rear. There was a red barn to the left of the driveway with a side door that led to a paddock.

Mr. Alltauk smoothed down the front of his suit. "Hello, hello!" he said, his face breaking into a nervous grin. He rushed to the passenger side of the car and held the door open while a slender woman got out. "How was your trip?"

Sure has big teeth, Becky thought, staring at his mouth.

"Fine," responded Mrs. Allison curiously. "Is everything all right?"

"Sure, sure." Mr. Alltauk pulled the collar away from his thin neck. "What I mean is, the people who used to live here moved out west, you know."

"We know," said Mrs. Allison, lifting a delicate hand to give the car door a shove. Her blue eyes took on a worried look. "Is anything wrong?"

"No, no," assured Mr. Alltauk quickly, his fingers fidgeting with his briefcase. "The only thing is, the girl who lives at the end of your lane has run into a few snags. It hasn't been easy." His smile was growing a little thin. "And now the people out west say there's nothing *they* can do about it," he finished, his voice fading at the end.

4

Mr. Allison frowned and ran his hand through his dark hair. "I'm afraid I'm not following you, Mr. Alltauk," he said. "What are you trying to tell us?"

"My, my, didn't I say?" The smile had disappeared. "I was talking about the ponies."

Mr. Allison shot a dismayed look at his wife as Becky pulled her eyes away from the real estate agent's teeth. "Ponies?" she asked. "I thought the ponies had gone."

Mr. Alltauk shook his head miserably as Becky ran toward the barn. She pushed the door open and slipped inside, then stood still for a moment allowing her eyes time to adjust to the dimness.

A wide aisle ran down the length of the barn with four stalls on the left. Across from the stalls and about halfway down the aisle stood a large, wooden tack trunk shoved up against the wall. Beyond the tack trunk was a door leading to the enclosed paddock.

From the first stall came the sound of rustling straw and a pony neighing softly. Becky stepped quickly down the aisle and peered over the door. The mare lifted her head, flaring her nostrils to take in the newcomer's scent. She was black in the front and back with a wide white stripe painted all the way around her middle.

"Hello," Becky said softly. "You look like an Oreo cookie."

"You got that right," came a voice from the next stall.

Becky caught her breath and whirled around. "Who's there?"

CHAPTER 2

No Job, No Ponies

The voice stepped into the aisle. "It's me, Amy Jo Ryan," she said, jabbing aimlessly at the straw with her pitchfork. "I live at the end of your lane." She nodded her head toward the black and white mare. "That pony belonged to the people who used to live here. Her name's Oreo," she explained. "Ginger's my pony. I was just tidying everything up a bit so it wouldn't look so messy when you got here."

"Oh," said Becky as she stretched her neck to look at the chestnut pony in the next stall. "I'm Becky Allison."

"Know anything about ponies?" asked Amy Jo nervously sizing up her new neighbor.

Becky blinked her eyes. "I used to take riding lessons at our old house."

Their conversation was interrupted by the sound of Mr. and Mrs. Allison's footsteps hurrying down the aisle.

"Now, Becky," Mr. Allison began, but stopped at the sight of another girl standing next to his daughter. She was small for her age, like his daughter, with large blue eyes, and auburn hair pulled back in a ponytail.

"Hi!" she said with a lopsided grin, then wiped the palms of her hands on the back of her jeans.

"This is Amy Jo Ryan," said Becky, introducing their new neighbor. "And this is my mom and dad. And, uh," she looked at her parents hopefully, "this is Oreo and the pony in the next stall is Ginger."

Mr. Allison shoved his hands in his pockets and glanced at his wife. "Well," he said, clearing his throat, "these ponies were supposed to be gone by the time we moved in." He looked at his fair-haired wife again, but she was busy petting Oreo. "Two ponies eat a lot," he continued, a frown creasing his forehead.

Amy Jo licked her lips quickly and plunged in. "I got it all figured out, Mr. Allison," she began. "Mrs. Davis runs the *Bedford Daily News*. She needs somebody to take over two paper routes, but it's too big for one person. So, here's the deal," she rushed on. "If Becky would help me, we could pay the ponies' expenses with the money we make delivering papers. Wouldn't cost you anything," she finished, her eyes darting back and forth between the two adults.

Becky studied her father, pressing her clasped hands to her mouth as she held her breath.

Mr. Allison rubbed the back of his neck. "I don't know, girls. Farrier has to shoe them about every six to eight weeks, vet bills, feed bills . . ."

"We'll work hard, Dad, I promise," pleaded Becky.

Mr. Allison raised his eyebrows as he looked at his wife who shrugged her shoulders as if to say, I don't see any way out of this. Leaning against the stall door he drew a line in the dirt floor with the edge of his shoe. He looked up and studied the two girls for a moment before making up his mind. "All right. We'll try it for a few months and see how it goes."

Becky ran forward, clasping her hands tightly behind her father's back. "Thanks, Dad!" she said, beaming up at him. "We'll take good care of them. I promise."

"Easy, you're knocking the wind out of me," he teased as a slow smile crept in around his eyes. "I know you will," he said softly.

He patted his daughter's shoulder and turned to his wife. "Okay, Evelyn, let's go tell Mr. Alltauk. Don't forget," he warned as he reached the door. "No job, no ponies."

Mrs. Allison chuckled as she followed her husband outside. "What happened to 'we're not keeping those ponies and that's final'?"

Becky shoved her hands into her pockets as she grinned at Amy Jo. "So, when do we start the paper route?"

"Uhh." Amy Jo looked at the ceiling. "The paper route," she repeated as she played with the latch on the stall door. "Well, it's like this," she continued, sweeping whispy bangs back with her forearm. "I haven't actually . . . what I mean is . . ."

Becky leaned forward studying Amy Jo's face. "We have the job, right?" she asked.

Amy Jo picked up the pitchfork and walked back into Ginger's stall. "Well, sorta yes and sorta no," she mumbled from the far corner of the stall.

Becky drew her eyebrows together. "Which part is sort of no?" she asked, resting her hand on Ginger's stall.

"The part that says I haven't talked to Mrs. Davis yet," she said. "But the good news is that she's always

9

looking for kids to deliver papers and I know for a fact that Jennie Michaels and Andi Howard are going on vacation for a few weeks."

Ginger stepped over and nosed Amy Jo's hand. "No carrots now, Ginger," she said softly, gently pushing the pony's head away. She gave a sidelong glance at her new neighbor. "She'll *probably* let us cover for them." Then added in a muffled voice, "If she can't find anybody else."

Becky blinked her eyes suspiciously. "Why wouldn't she give us the job?" she asked. "Doesn't she like you or something?"

Amy Jo flipped and reflipped the same pile of straw. "It's not that she doesn't *like* me, exactly."

Becky waited a few seconds for an explanation. "What's the problem, then, *exactly*?"

Amy Jo stopped digging with her pitchfork and turned to Becky. "I'm definitely experienced. I had Jennie's paper route last year," she explained, then began to smooth her pony's mane. "I got the papers delivered on time, usually. A couple times I didn't see the storm clouds." She drew her lips together. "People can get awful fussy about wet papers. But, other than that, things weren't too bad." Amy Jo shrugged her shoulders. "Anyway, that's not my main job, but my main job doesn't pay anything."

Becky tilted her head. "You have a job?" she asked. "How old are you?"

Amy Jo stretched up her shoulders. "Eleven," she said, arching her eyebrows.

Becky looked puzzled. "That's how old I am and you already have a job? Where do you work?"

"Well, I don't actually work *at* a place," Amy Jo began. "You see, I'm a detective."

"A detective?!" Becky's eyes grew wide. "Why would a little village the size of Bedford need a detective?" she asked.

Amy Jo looked over her shoulder, then leaned closer. "You wouldn't believe some of the things that go on around here," she said knowingly as she nodded her head. "I kinda think of myself as a young Sherlock Holmes. You've heard of him, right?"

Becky nodded her head, her mouth slightly ajar.

Amy Jo took a deep breath, leaned against the stall, and crossed her arms. "Arthur Conan Doyle wrote lots of detective stories about Sherlock Holmes. He had a sidekick, Dr. Watson. They worked tons of cases together, but Mr. Holmes was the real detective."

"I know who they are," said Becky. "We've seen Sherlock Holmes on TV. My dad has the books."

Amy Jo nodded her head, impressed. "Okay, well, actually, I've got a bunch of detective equipment at my house. My dad was a detective and he had a lab in the basement. I use some of his stuff sometimes to help solve my cases."

"Don't your parents worry about all this detective business?" asked Becky.

Amy Jo looked down and began to finger the end of her belt. "There's just my mom and me. My dad died two years ago when I was in fourth grade."

Becky blinked her eyes a few times as she stared at Amy Jo. "I'm sorry," she finally said.

Amy Jo wrapped her arms around Ginger's neck and kissed her face. "That's okay; you didn't know," she said softly.

Becky chewed the bottom of her lip and stared at Oreo. The mare squeezed her nose as far as she could through the slats of the door and licked Becky's arm.

A smile played on Amy Jo's lips. She walked over to a small bin next to the tack trunk, lifted the lid, and picked out three large carrots. "She wants a treat," she explained.

"Thanks," said Becky. She kept her eyes lowered as she took the carrots from Amy Jo, then unlatched the stall door and stepped inside.

Amy Jo watched, with approval, as Oreo and her new neighbor made friends. "I'll call Mrs. Davis at the newspaper when I go home," she began. "I look at it this way. There aren't many kids around here looking for a paper route for the summer anyway, so she'll probably give us the job."

Becky broke off another piece of carrot. "If she does give us the job, when do you think we'll start?"

"We'd have to start at the end of this week when Jennie and Andi leave for the shore."

"What time do the papers have to be delivered?"

Amy Jo's eyes lit up mischievously. "How often have you seen the sun rise?" she asked.

Becky looked up in surprise. "Not often, why?"

Amy Jo gave her a look that said, just wait. "Well, you're going to see it clear the horizon plenty now."

Becky leaned against the wall. "Every day?!"

"Not every day," began Amy Jo with a grin. "We get Sundays off."

CHAPTER 3

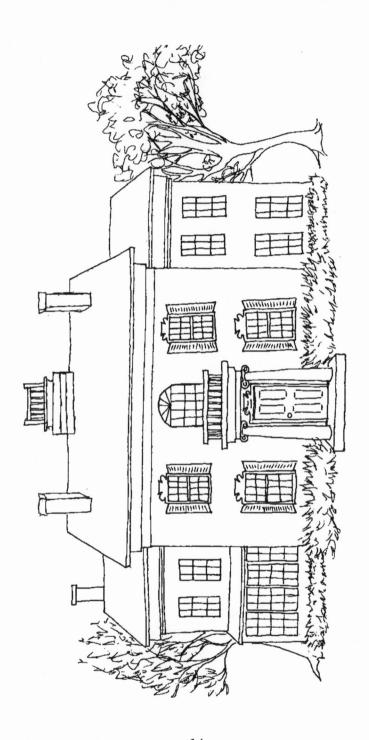

Mrs. Martin's House

In the predawn light, Becky yawned as she sat cross legged folding newspapers beside Amy Jo's house. She looked up and squinted. Through the mist, she could just make out the squarish outline of her house back the lane. Beside her, Amy Jo had finished folding her share and was stacking them in her saddlebag.

Amy Jo eyed her new friend impatiently. "People can get real snippy if they don't have the morning paper when their coffee gets ready, so you'd better hurry up," she warned as she pulled herself into the saddle. Ginger snorted and backed up. The morning air was crisp and cool and she pawed the ground, eager to get started.

"Last one," Becky announced, stretching a rubber band over the folded paper. She gathered up her newspapers, hauled them over to her new pony, and stuffed them into her saddlebag. Oreo side stepped, knocking Becky off balance just as she placed her foot in the stirrup. "Whoa, girl! Hold still!" she said, giving the reins a little jerk. "How do you know which houses get the morning paper?" she asked, once in the saddle.

"The first part of the paper route is the same as I had last year. I used to sub for Andi, so I know her route, too," Amy Jo called over her shoulder. "I'll show you the whole route for now. But after next week we'll split it up and I'll take one side of the road and you can take the other side. We'll get done faster that way." Amy Jo looked at her confidently. "You'll know it by then."

Becky frowned doubtfully. "Okay," she said as she guided Oreo to the right side of Ginger.

As they came to the first driveway, Amy Jo drew back on her reins. "Now take Mr. Finkleberger, for instance," she said, taking his paper out of her saddlebag. "He's the cranky type. But if you deliver his paper on time every day, sometimes he twists his mouth a little bit like he's smiling at you."

Becky nodded her head as she looked up at the faded, yellow house set back behind a ragged row of hedges. From the window she saw the outline of a thin, bald, round-headed little man sipping from a mug.

Amy Jo stuffed the newspaper into the container beside his mailbox reserved for the *Bedford Daily News*, then crossed to the other side of the road.

Becky leaned over and read the name on the mailbox. "Finster."

"Yeah, I see them at Hank's Ice Cream Store in Bedford with their three little kids sometimes." Amy Jo pulled a face. "They're cute, but they think they can hang all over me just because I deliver their papers."

They trudged along silently until they came to a mailbox labeled "Martin." "My favorite customer," said

Amy Jo as they rode past the mailbox. "We're old buddies."

Becky turned and glanced at the Martin mailbox as they rode by it. "If she's one of your customers, how come you're not putting the newspaper in the box?" she asked.

"She's pretty old so I take her paper right up to the door," Amy Jo explained as she guided Ginger down a long driveway. "Besides, she often leaves chocolate chip cookies for me," she confided sheepishly.

"Does she live alone?" asked Becky.

"Her husband died a long time ago, but she usually has somebody living with her to help her out," said Amy Jo. "This house has been in her family for a long time. Her dad didn't trust banks so he always kept a lot of money stashed around the house somewhere," she informed her friend. "Actually, I hear Mrs. Martin does the same thing, only she's always changing the hiding place." Amy Jo shook her head. "My mom worries that someday she'll forget where the money is hidden. She calls her an eccentric."

Becky looked quizzically at her new friend. "What's an eccentric?" she asked.

"Uh," Amy Jo drew her eyebrows together trying to remember, "I think it's somebody who doesn't act like everybody else." She thought for a moment then nodded her head.

Becky thought about that for a moment then asked, "How about Mrs. Martin? Doesn't she trust anybody with her money either?"

Amy Jo took a deep breath and let it out slowly. "I don't think so," she decided. "Sometimes she invited me into the house. But when I collected for the newspaper I had to wait outside. She'd dig the money out of wherever she had hidden it that day and bring it out to me."

Additions had been built onto both sides of the large, brick, two-storied house and there was a covered stoop leading to the door. Outbuildings in need of a hammer and paintbrush were scattered to the side and back of the property.

Amy Jo grabbed a paper from her saddlebag, slid down from her pony, and walked up the front step. She was about to lay the newspaper down when a small, gray-haired lady opened the door.

"Why, hello, Amy Jo." Mrs. Martin smiled in surprise. Her pale, deeply veined hand trembled slightly as she reached up and fondly brushed Amy Jo's bangs out of her eyes.

Amy Jo grinned back at her old friend. "Hi, Mrs. Martin," she said.

Mrs. Martin clasped her hands together. "I didn't know you were taking over Jennie's route." Then glancing over Amy Jo's shoulder at Ginger. "And you still ride your dear little pony to deliver newspapers."

Amy Jo nodded her head. "Yep, still riding Ginger," she said, gazing fondly at her mare. "Jennie and Andi are gone for the summer. We needed to make some money, so I asked Mrs. Davis for my old job back," she explained, then turned so that Mrs. Martin could see her partner. "This is my new neighbor, Becky Allison. We're going to be delivering papers together."

"Oh," Mrs. Martin raised her hand slightly in a wave and laughed lightly. "You two young people will help keep each other company delivering papers. I'll have to remember to put some extra cookies in the bag." She placed her hands together and gave Amy Jo a knowing smile.

The early morning breeze pressed Mrs. Martin's dress around her frail body. "So, how have you been, Mrs. Martin," asked Amy Jo, glancing at the sunken hollow of the old woman's throat.

"Not so good," replied Mrs. Martin, shaking her head. "I called Mrs. Davis and put an ad in the paper last week for some help. Can't manage otherwise. The Emersons were with me for a long time, you know, but they had to retire. I'm so close to the village someone could even walk here."

"Is there anything we can do for you?" Becky offered.

Mrs. Martin smiled in gratitude. "It's awfully sweet of you to ask, but I need somebody big to do some heavy work outside," she sighed. "I can't keep this place going for long by myself."

"Hm," Amy Jo's brows knitted together as she studied Mrs. Martin's face. "I sure hope you find somebody real soon," she said.

"Things aren't as bad as all that," said Mrs. Martin, smoothing the worried look from her young friend's forehead. "I just talked to a woman over the phone last night who's willing to do some cooking and cleaning for me. Her name's Maggie . . . something," she frowned in thought. Then looking vacantly into space she continued. "I would just hate to give up my home."

Amy Jo nodded her head sympathetically, then turned and walked down the step. "If there's anything we can do, just give us a call."

Mrs. Martin smiled at the offer. "Thank you, Amy Jo, but I'll be all right."

"It was nice meeting you, Mrs. Martin," said Becky politely as they turned their ponies to leave.

"Welcome to Bedford," replied Mrs. Martin. "I'm sure you'll enjoy your new home."

As they neared the entrance to the road, an old dusty truck pulled into the driveway. The words "Jim's Paint and Repair Service" were written on the side. Becky raised her hand and waved, but the stranger lowered his head and pulled his gray hat down farther over his eyebrows.

"Hm," said Becky, turning around in her saddle, "I wonder if he's applying for the job Mrs. Martin advertised in the paper?"

Amy Jo eyed the license plate on the back of the disappearing truck. *Hm, out-of-state tags,* she thought. "I don't know," she said, facing the front again. "He's not very friendly."

Becky shrugged her shoulders. "Maybe he didn't see us," she suggested.

Amy Jo eyed her friend. "Or maybe he doesn't want to be seen."

"What do you mean?"

Amy Jo thought for a moment. "He pulled his hat down on his head as soon as he saw us," she decided. "Anyway, it's awful early in the morning to be applying for a job."

Becky grinned. "Your detective brain  is working overtime."

"Maybe," said Amy Jo doubtfully, shifting forward in her saddle.

CHAPTER 4

Siren-Red

As the 5:30 alarm rattled the darkened room, Amy Jo pulled the sheet over her head and groaned. *Whose idea was this anyway*, she thought to herself as she staggered across the room to shut the annoying thing off. She splashed cold water on her face and stared at herself in the mirror through drooping eyelids. She'd already learned that if she went back to bed for a few seconds she'd fall asleep. Then Becky, ticked as all get out, would ride down the lane and throw pebbles at her window until she got up. Last time that happened, she threw on a pair of too short jeans and a wrong-side-out T-shirt before flying out the door. Getting the ponies to cooperate that early in the morning was another matter.

"Oh, come on, Oreo," Becky urged. "We'll get these papers delivered and then I'll give you some nice hay and grain," she promised as she slipped the bridle over her pony's shaking head. "Maybe even a few carrots if you're good."

Amy Jo rubbed her eyes and yawned. "I know how they feel," she said, laying her head on top of Ginger's back. "Maybe we can take a little snooze when we get done."

"Fine example you set," said Becky, tightening the girth around Oreo's stomach. "You're talking Ginger right back into a nap. Anyway, I'm ready to leave and you haven't even started yet."

"Okay, I'm awake now," said Amy Jo, opening one eye.

Becky grabbed Ginger's bridle while Amy Jo picked out her pony's hoofs. "Come on, Ginger, open your mouth wider," said Becky as she slipped her finger in the corner of the pony's mouth.

"So, what do you think?" asked Amy Jo as they stuffed the last of the folded papers into their saddlebags. Do you know the route well enough to go on your own today?"

Becky nodded. "Sure, I can do it," she answered confidently.

Amy Jo lifted her arm and pointed to the right side of the road. "Okay, you take Mr. Finkleberger's side of the road and I'll take Mrs. Martin's side."

Becky placed her hands on her hips and gave her friend a look that said, how come I get Mr. Finkleberger's side and you get Mrs. Martin's side?

Amy Jo waved a hand aside. "Don't worry," she assured her friend. "I'll save half the cookies for you."

Ginger was on auto pilot. She knew the entire route by heart and stopped at every mailbox that got a newspaper without having to be reined in. By the time they reached Mrs. Martin's driveway the mare down-shifted to the right.

As her mistress slid down from the saddle and approached the door, Ginger hung her head and lowered her lids. The Martin house usually meant nap time.

The front door opened and Amy Jo gasped. Even Ginger did a double take. Siren-red hair. Amy Jo had seen the color on the dye bottle at the drug store. She knew it was bad manners to stare, but she wasn't even thinking in that direction. *Got to be Maggie*, she thought. Dark circles hung like half moons under the woman's eyes. *I'm tired, too, but she looks like she hasn't slept in a week.*

The woman squinted her eyes 'til they were nearly closed. "Look," she said, tossing a hand in the direction of the driveway, "you can just put the paper in the box beside the road from now on. I'll walk down for it."

Amy Jo squinted her eyes in return and nodded her head. *Definitely siren-red.* "Well, I always bring the newspaper to the house," she explained, focusing her attention back to the woman's face. "Are you Maggie?" she finally asked.

The woman folded her arms and leaned against the door frame. "Yeah, I just got here. It's my first day. Just put it in the box by the road, I'll get it," she repeated, then stepped back inside the house and closed the door.

Amy Jo stood motionless, staring at the front door. She cocked her head to the side and frowned then retraced her steps to Ginger's side. "Well, well, what do you think of that?" she asked, stroking her pony's muzzle. "Do you get the feeling we're not wanted around here?"

At the edge of the lawn, came the sound of hammering.

Amy Jo pulled the reins over Ginger's head and pulled the reluctant pony in the direction of the dusty truck. *Sorta tall and skinny*, thought Amy Jo eyeing the handyman. "Hi, Jim!" she said, glancing at the name on the truck.

Jim started and lowered his hammer, then turned around, a crease forming between his eyes. "Hello," he said, pulling his gray hat lower over his forehead.

"So," Amy Jo began, licking her lips, "how are you?"

Jim let the hammer slip between his fingers. "Fine," he answered, staring at the ground, his hat shielding his face from her gaze.

"Good," she commented, ducking her head down a bit to catch his expression.

Amy Jo licked her lips again. "How's the work going?" she pressed, glancing over her shoulder at the door to the house.

"All right," he answered shortly. When Jim leaned over to pull a weed from the ground, a letter fell from his shirt pocket and landed near Amy Jo's feet. As she stooped to picked it up, Jim stepped forward and snatched it out of her hands before she could return it to him.

His left jaw muscle worked as he unfolded the letter. "Is there something you want?" he asked curtly.

Amy Jo frowned, staring at the letter. "No, not really," she said as she watched Jim gaze at its contents. "Not exactly," she stalled, leaning forward and arching her neck. As he refolded the letter, she settled back on her heels. "Well, sort of," she finally admitted.

Jim pressed his narrow lips together and returned the letter to his pocket, buttoning it this time for security. "Could you make it short, I'm busy right now."

"Oh, sure, sure," she stammered. "I just wondered if you knew anything about Mrs. Martin's new maid, Maggie."

Jim looked at her for a second then  reached down and picked up his hammer. "No," he said abruptly as he returned to his work.

Amy Jo rolled her eyes. *I get it, it's a contest to see which one of you can be the rudest*, she thought to herself, then said. "Gotta run, bye."

"Right," Jim answered without turning around.

*   *   *   *

Becky and Oreo stood waiting at the end of the driveway as Amy Jo and Ginger ambled toward the road.

"How did it go?" asked Amy Jo, scowling at the ground.

"I think I forgot somebody," Becky reported. "I have a paper left over."

Amy Jo nodded her head. "Great, let's head back."

Becky turned in her saddle and looked closely at her friend. "Actually, I didn't deliver any papers at all; I made a big pile and burned them all."

"Good," murmured Amy Jo. "We're all set."

"Amy Jo!" said Becky in an exasperated voice.

Amy Jo jumped and Ginger shied to the side, nearly knocking her rider off.

"What'd you do that for?!" asked Amy Jo, pulling back on the reins and tightening her legs.

"You haven't been listening to a word I've said."

Amy Jo returned Becky's glare. "What are you talking about?" she asked angrily.

Becky's shoulders dropped and she looked away, then turned quickly back. "I said I had one paper left over."

Amy Jo sat up in her saddle and turned Ginger around. "Well, why didn't you say so in the first place," she replied. "We've got to go back and find out who you missed."

Becky opened her mouth to respond then dropped the reins as she threw up her hands. When Oreo felt the reins flap against her neck, she took a step forward. Becky quickly gathered up the reins and fell into step with Ginger. "What were you thinking about?" she asked her friend.

Amy Jo's eyes grew thoughtful. "I'll tell you something, Beck. They're acting weird at Mrs. Martin's house."

"Like how?" asked Becky, a puzzled look on her face.

"Maggie's the new maid Mrs. Martin hired and she told me not to deliver the paper to the house anymore."

"Maybe she wants to save you the ride down the driveway," suggested Becky.

"Maybe," said Amy Jo doubtfully. "Except, Jim acted sort of weird, too."

"Who's Jim?"

"He's the handyman we saw the first day. You remember the guy in the old, dusty truck?"

"Oh, yeah," said Becky, then shook her head. "You oughta give this detective thing a rest," she advised.

"There was this letter," Amy Jo began, giving Becky a wilting look. "It dropped out of his pocket and all I did was try to pick it up for him," she said, giving a short, curt laugh. "The way he acted you'd have thought

I snatched some secret document out of his  safe and tried to read it."

Becky looked over teasingly. "Well, would you have read it?"

For a moment, Amy Jo lifted her chin and eyebrows. Then looked over at her friend and grinned. "Only if he wasn't looking," she admitted.

*　　*　　*　　*

"Uh oh," Amy Jo muttered under her breath as the outline of a bald, round-headed man came into view. He had his arm slung over the mailbox and was tapping the top of it with his fingertips.

"Mr. Finkleberger doesn't look too happy," said Becky, pulling her hard hat lower on her forehead."

"He was your first one!" hissed Amy Jo. "How could you have missed him?"

Becky hunched down lower in her saddle. "Well, I just did, that's all," she hissed back, allowing Oreo to fall behind Ginger.

Amy Jo drew in her reins, smiled feebly, and handed Mr. Finkleberger the morning newspaper. "Sorry," was all she could eke out.

Mr. Finkleberger whipped the paper out of her hand, leaned around Ginger, and gave Becky a hard look. "Mrs. Davis shall hear of this!" he threatened, then cinched the belt around his bathrobe tighter, pivoted on the heel of his slipper, and marched back to the house.

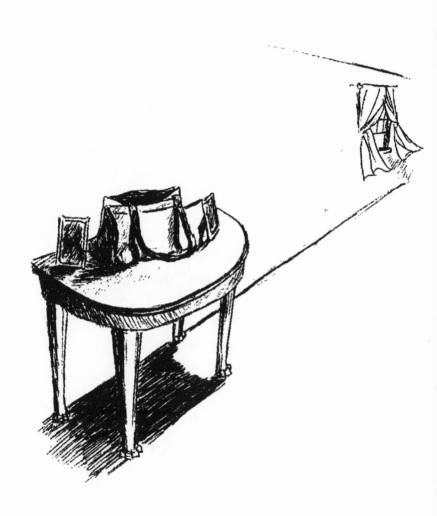

CHAPTER 5

The Money's Missing

"Got enough change?" asked Amy Jo as they rode out of the lane together the following week.

Becky patted her side pocket. "Right here," she said.

"Good," Amy Jo nodded. "We have to give the money to Mrs. Davis by the first of the month, so I always collect a few days before that in case somebody's not home, then it gives me a couple more days to catch them." She thought a moment. "I hope you don't have a bunch of people giving you a ten dollar bill or you'll run out of change."

"Hm," said Becky, "I hope not, too, because I didn't bring *that* much change with me."

As they reached Mr. Finkleberger's house, they saw that his drapes were pulled tightly shut.

"Happens every collection day," sighed Amy Jo, shaking her head.

"It wasn't just for the cookies that you gave me this side of the road, was it?" said Becky accusingly.

Amy Jo let her breath out slowly. "Well, you only missed him one time; he'll get over it," she said quickly. "Anyway, this gives me an excuse to ride up to Mrs. Martin's house and check on her," she added quickly, then kicked Ginger into a canter. "See ya back at the barn."

A car was parked beside Jim's truck as Amy Jo rode into Mrs. Martin's driveway. A dent was visible on the rear door and the side window was taped over with plastic.

Amy Jo gazed at it for a moment, then nudged Ginger forward to the hitching post. She stepped up to the door and knocked. She was about to knock again when she heard footsteps approaching. It was Maggie, but she was opening the door to allow a woman in a pale blue uniform to leave.

The woman was shorter and heavier than Maggie and quite a bit older. A nurse's cap was jammed on top of gray hair that was pulled tightly back. She looked startled to see someone on the other side of the door.

Maggie frowned for a moment, then asked with a tired voice. "What is it?"

Amy Jo looked from Maggie to the other woman and back. "I'm here to collect for the newspaper and I need to see Mrs. Martin," she explained.

Maggie placed her hands on her hips as she stared at Amy Jo, then turned to the other woman. "What do you think, Miss Windle?" she asked.

Miss Windle leaned forward until her face was only a few inches from Amy Jo. She inspected the girl through bifocal lenses with dark eyes that seemed twice their normal size. Her left eyeball scowled into Amy Jo's face while the right one looked off to the side.

The nurse wrinkled her nose distastefully. "Children can be very tiring," she said with a squeaky sort of voice, "but if she only stays for a few minutes, I suppose it'll be all right." She straightened up, smoothed down her starched uniform, and turned back to Maggie. "I have to see another patient on the other side of the village right now. I'll be back tomorrow," she continued unblinkingly. Then, with a jerk of her head, she walked upright and shoulders back towards her car.

Amy Jo's eyes flickered between the rusty, dented car with the patched window and Miss Windle's rigid back. *They're an odd match*, she thought.

"Come along then," said Maggie, calling Amy Jo's attention back to the house.

Amy Jo trailed after Maggie down the length of the hallway. "What's wrong with Mrs. Martin?" she asked, trying to keep up.

Maggie turned without warning. Amy Jo nearly collided into her. "She had a blood clot in her brain and suffered a small stroke three days ago," she explained. "The doctor let her come home, but Miss Windle has to come every day to check on her." Maggie opened her mouth to say something, then shook her head and continued up to the landing.

Amy Jo frowned. *What was all that about*, she thought, rushing to catch up. At the second step, her foot caught on the carpet and she stumbled forward. Amy Jo looked up quickly, but Maggie had crossed the landing and was out of sight. Reaching out, Amy Jo grabbed the banister. She pulled herself up and hurried to join Mrs. Martin's maid outside the bedroom door.

"Don't stay long," warned Maggie as she opened the bedroom door. Amy Jo edged passed her and the door was quietly closed.

A pile of blankets covered Mrs. Martin's thin body. *Must be eighty degrees in here*, thought Amy Jo, wiping her forehead.

The old woman opened her eyes and smiled weakly. "Hello, Amy Jo. It seems like a lot of medicine, doesn't it?" she said, following her young friend's glance at the dark bottles lined up on her night stand.

"Hi, Mrs. Martin," said Amy Jo softly as she walked to the side of the bed. "How are you? Do you need to take all that stuff?" she asked, still eyeing the bottles.

Mrs. Martin nodded sadly. "I feel groggy a lot, especially in the afternoon and evening. I try to get up a little bit every morning, but it's not easy to get around. I can't seem to remember a lot of things," Mrs. Martin admitted vaguely, then gave a small chuckle. "The nurse has threatened to move in if I don't get better soon. Right now she stops by every day to give me my medicine and check on me."

Mrs. Martin looked at the bag Amy Jo always carried over her shoulder whenever she collected. "How much do I owe you, dear?" she asked.

Amy Jo's face flushed pink as she looked down at her collection bag. "It's for the whole month, but I can come back when you're feeling better, Mrs. Martin," she said, backing towards the door. "I don't want you to worry about that now."

Mrs. Martin smiled faintly at her friend's concern. "Just give me my handbag," she said, her limp hand directing Amy Jo to a table by the window. Amy Jo hesitated and looked down at her boots. "It's all right, dear, just bring it here," Mrs. Martin assured her.

Amy Jo walked over to the table, picked up the handbag, and placed it carefully on the bed.

Mrs. Martin pulled out her billfold, opened it up, and frowned. She drew the handbag onto her lap and searched through it as well. "I was sure . . ." she began,

pressing fingertips to her trembling lips. She
put the billfold down on the bed. Her head
dropped back onto the pillow and she closed
her eyes. "Let me think a minute," she whispered.

Amy Jo studied Mrs. Martin, exhaustion etched
around her friend's eyes. "Mrs. Martin," she began softly,
"really it doesn't matter. I can come back."

Mrs. Martin opened her eyes and stared at the ceiling. "I just don't understand it," she said frowning. "I thought
I took one hundred dollars out of my money box last week,
but now the money's missing." She closed her eyes again
and moved her head side to side. "I can't remember where I
put my money box this time," she worried. A tear trickled
down the side of her face. "I need to find it."

"Please don't worry about it," pleaded Amy Jo.
"Maybe I can help you find it."

Mrs. Martin opened her eyes. "I don't know where
to tell you to start looking," she said, feeling helpless
and confused.

Amy Jo gently placed her hand over the sick
woman's arm. "It'll be all right, Mrs. Martin," she
assured her friend, then asked, "Would you like for me
to put your handbag back on the table?"

When Mrs. Martin nodded, Amy Jo put the billfold back in the handbag, clicked the clasp shut, and
placed it on the table. "Can I get you something, Mrs.
Martin?" asked Amy Jo quietly.

"Just open the window a little bit before you leave,
dear. A little fresh air in the room would be nice," said
Mrs. Martin, her eyes closed again.

Amy Jo walked over to the window, unlocked the
catch at the top, and lifted it a couple of inches, then

turned around and stared at her friend. "I'll see you later," she said softly as she walked slowly to the door.

Amy Jo stood outside Mrs. Martin's room for a moment with her hand on the doorknob. She heard noises coming from the kitchen below where the maid was working. "Hm," she said to herself as walked down the stairs. "It has to be somebody who can go in and out of the house without making anybody suspicious. But how did the thief take the money out of Mrs. Martin's handbag without her seeing it?"

CHAPTER 6

The Wicked Witch of the West

Becky leaned against the door in Ginger's stall and watched Amy Jo toss the dirty straw three feet beyond the muck bucket. "So, what are you going to do?" she asked as she watched a growing pile of straw mount in front of her feet.

Amy Jo leaned against the pitchfork as she caught her breath. "Look," she began, pushing her damp bangs aside, "some money's been stolen, a money box is missing, and there are some suspicious characters hanging around Mrs. Martin's house. Now, Sherlock Holmes and Dr. Watson would be doing something about it."

Becky stared at her for a second. "Maybe so, but I'm not Dr. Watson and I don't know anything about detectiving," she finished.

"It's a cinch," Amy Jo shook her head. "I'll teach you everything you need to know."

Becky stared at the floor for a long moment, then looked up to meet Amy Jo's steady gaze. "Okay," she said rather nervously, "so what do we do?"

Amy Jo smiled her thanks, put her pitchfork aside, and began pacing back and forth in the aisle. "I've been thinking about this ever since I talked with Mrs. Martin and I've got a plan."

"What sort of plan?" asked Becky as her eyes followed her friend.

Amy Jo stopped in front of Becky and took a deep breath. "First, we need to find where Mrs. Martin hid her money box," she said as she ticked off one finger. "Second, somebody took some money out of her billfold, I'm sure of it. We've got it narrowed down to three suspects, but we don't know which one of the three, right?"

"I haven't been over there for a couple of weeks. Which three people are you talking about?" asked Becky.

Amy Jo sighed in exasperation. "Right, I forgot. Jim is the handyman; you saw him the first day we delivered papers."

Becky nodded her head.

"Maggie's the maid and Miss Windle's the nurse. Got it?"

"Got it," said Becky.

Amy Jo chewed on her lip as she thought. "What I need is some excuse to go into the house. First, to look

38

for the money box and second to plant some marked money in her handbag."

Becky blinked several times then asked, "How are you going to mark the money?"

"I'll take a black pen and mark the first and last zero in the serial number of each ten dollar bill," she began. "I thought about using red ink, but that might stand out too much. They won't notice black as much."

"But how are you going to know if somebody takes the money?"

Amy Jo smiled knowingly. "We'll stake out the house and tail anybody who leaves and goes into the village. If he buys something using the marked money, we'll know he's the thief," she finished, then shoved her hands in her pockets and rocked back and forth on her heels. "Well? What do you think of my idea?"

Becky stared at Amy Jo in amazement. "'Stake out'? 'Tail'?" she said, scratching her head. "I'm in over my head already."

Amy Jo pulled a face. "It's no big deal. Anyway, Mrs. Martin only lives two blocks out of town," she reminded her friend. "We'll hide behind the trees across the road from the driveway and follow whoever pulls out. If the person spends any of the marked money in the village, we'll call in the police."

Becky's eyes widened. "Police?" she repeated to herself, then asked. "Where are you going to get the ten dollar bills?"

"From the paper route money."

Becky's mouth dropped open. "The paper route money!? That's for the ponies' feed," she said, placing her hands on her hips. "What if you lose the suspect?"

"Suspect?!" Amy Jo grinned. "I love it! You're talking like a real detective now."

Becky's eyes narrowed. "It's not funny."

"Okay, okay," said Amy Jo, holding up her hands. "I promise to stick to the suspects like glue. I will not let anyone escape with our paper route money, cross my heart and hope to die."

Becky looked unconvinced, but let the issue slide.

Amy Jo frowned. "Now, the question is, how do we get past the front door so I can plant the money in Mrs. Martin's handbag?"

Becky folded her arms and hung her head as Amy Jo began pacing again. "Maybe we could bake her some cookies," she suggested, turning to her new partner. "It'd be a switch from her always baking cookies for us."

Amy Jo stopped dead and looked up. "That's a great idea! We'll take the cookies over, ask to see Mrs. Martin, and stick the money in her handbag . . . no sweat."

Amy Jo trotted for the barn door with Becky hard on her heels, then dragged her beat-up bike from behind the bushes. "I'll go home and mark the money. How much time do you need to get the cookies ready?" she asked, her foot on the pedal.

Becky stood there and sucked in her breath, feeling as though she was being drawn under by quicksand. "Couple of hours maybe," she said.

"Good," said Amy Jo, checking her watch. "I'll be back with the money then."

*　　*　　*　　*

As soon as Becky saw her friend toss her bike behind the bushes, she grabbed her saddlebag with the cookies inside and headed out the back door. "Right here." She patted the saddlebag in answer to Amy Jo's raised eyebrows.

"Okay, Ginger, time to go to work," called Amy Jo as she marched down the aisle. The chestnut mare walked around her stall playing hard to get. "Come on, Ginger. I know you thought you were done for the day, but we've got a job to do."

The pony laid her ears back, put her head in the corner, and turned her back end to Amy Jo.

"Pouting isn't going to get you anywhere, Ginger," she said as she walked around to the corner and slipped the bridle over her pony's head.

Becky leveled her eyes between the slats in the stall door and saw a sleeping Oreo laying on her side. "Her eyes are shut," she said, filled with hope. "I hate waking her up; maybe we should wait until tomorrow."

"Oh, she's probably faking it just to get out of work," said Amy Jo. "Walk over and rattle the carrot bin. That'll get her up."

Becky gave Amy Jo a doubtful look, but walked over and shook the carrot bin anyway. Oreo popped up and nickered through the slats of her stall door.

"Told ya," said Amy Jo.

Becky sighed, shrugged her shoulders, and muttered, "Oh, well, looks like there's no way out of this."

*   *   *   *

"Maggie's never seen you before because I deliver papers on that side of the road," Amy Jo began as they rode down the lane. "You stay back in the bushes and hold the ponies while I go up to the house."

"What's the fact that Maggie's never seen me before got to do with anything?" asked Becky.

"I might need to use you later on if Plan A doesn't work out," Amy Jo explained. "And it'll be important for her to think that we're not together."

With the house nearly in sight, the girls heard the sound of a car door slam and an engine start. They hopped off their ponies and hurried them inside the protective cover of trees and bushes just as the car neared their hiding place. With one hand over their ponies' muzzles, they reached in front and eased a limb aside.

It was the rusty, dented car from yesterday. Miss Windle's hawkish nose was an inch from the steering wheel as she scowled through the windshield. Seconds later, she was on the road driving towards the village.

"Do you remember the Wicked Witch of the West in *The Wizard of Oz*?" asked Amy Jo, shaking her head.

Becky looked at her friend and giggled. She could see it coming. "Yeah, why?"

Amy Jo nodded her head in the direction of the road. "Well, that's who Miss Windle reminds me of."

Becky stopped laughing as she thought of Amy Jo's old friend. "Poor Mrs. Martin," she said sympa-

42

thetically as her friend dug out the cookies and marched off towards the house.

Amy Jo took a deep breath, stepped up to the porch, and knocked on the door. As she waited for someone to answer, she turned around and gave a small thumbs-up sign in the direction of the trees where Becky was waiting. She turned around as the door opened. It was Siren-Red.

The woman squinted at Amy Jo as though she'd never seen her before. "What do you want?" she asked in a hurried voice.

"I thought maybe Mrs. Martin might like some cookies so we, I mean so I made some for her," Amy Jo began cautiously. "Thought maybe it might make her feel better."

Maggie glanced back over her shoulder quickly, then stepped forward, using her body as a shield against the door's opening. "The nurse said she can't see anybody for a while."

"What do you mean?" asked Amy Jo in alarm. "Is she worse?"

"No, but Miss Windle said Mrs. Martin gets confused and upset when people ask her things she can't remember, so she's not allowed to see anybody until she gets better." Maggie held out her hand. "You better give them to me; I'll take them up to her."

Amy Jo stood up straight and narrowed her eyes. "Just ask Mrs. Martin if I can come in for a minute," she insisted. "She'll see me."

Maggie stood up a little straighter, too. "I told you, she can't see anybody right now," she answered, still holding out her hand. "Now, if you want her to have the cookies, you'll have to give them to *me*."

Amy Jo pressed her lips together, then reluctantly handed over the bag of cookies. Maggie took the bag, walked inside, and shut the door.

"Plan B," muttered Amy Jo as she turned and stepped off the porch. She stuck her hands in her pocket and kicked the stones on the driveway as she walked back to where Becky was holding the ponies.

"Can't see her. Nurse says she can't have visitors," she muttered, scowling over her shoulder at the house. "Maggie's probably making the whole thing up. She's trying to keep me out of the house for some reason."

Becky studied her friend for a moment. "You know there's always a chance she's telling the truth."

"That's a laugh," scoffed Amy Jo. "She's probably got the whole place torn up looking for the money."

The girls mounted their ponies and ambled toward the road. "Well, that finishes that," said Becky, turning to looked at her friend. "Nice try, but it didn't work."

Amy Jo shot a quick glance at Becky. "You think I'm giving up after the first try?"

Becky looked over in surprise. "What can we do now?"

"Plan B," said Amy Jo, forcefully.

Becky looked over doubtfully. "Plan B?"

"Yeah, Plan B," answered Amy Jo. "We'll go back again tonight."

"I don't think so. She already said you couldn't go inside," Becky reminded her friend. "She's not going to change her mind by tonight."

Becky twisted her mouth back and forth a few times, then gave her friend a sidelong glance. *Looks like her jaw's set in stone,* she thought. "Okay, what's Plan B?" she asked, sighing.

Amy Jo smiled slyly. "Okay, we'll both go there tonight, but you'll be at the front door keeping Maggie busy while I sneak around to the back."

CHAPTER 7

Girl Scout Cookies

The sun was low in the horizon as they parted the shrubs bordering Mrs. Martin's property. The glare from the setting sun kept anyone in the house from seeing the girls hiding behind the bushes.

Becky's eyes darted nervously over her shoulder. "Why did I ever agree to do this?" she worried.

Amy Jo ignored Becky as she sat on her haunches. "Maggie's probably got her locked up in her room . . ." she began, "punching her around trying to find out where she hides the money box." Her fiery eyes studied the house. "Maybe she's even got a wall safe behind a picture just full of valuables and Maggie's trying to get the combination. Only it's Mrs. Martin's life savings and she's bravely hanging on until she's rescued."

Becky stopped feeling nervous as she stared, mouth agape, at Amy Jo. "You must be nuts!" she finally said.

Amy Jo pressed her lips together as she turned to her friend. "Who knows what's going on inside that house?!" she said in exasperation. "Now, look, this is what we're going to do," she continued as she placed her hand on Becky's shoulder. "Maggie's never seen you before, so you go up and knock on the door and keep her talking while I slip around to the back of the house."

47

"Knock on the door and keep her talking?!" asked Becky, wide-eyed with astonishment. "I can't think of one thing to talk about."

Amy Jo squeezed her lower lip between her thumb and finger. "Hm," she thought, then jerked her head up, "tell her you're a Girl Scout selling cookies."

Becky extended her empty hands. "But I don't *have* any cookies. Girl Scouts always bring samples of cookies and order forms or *something*."

Amy Jo frowned for a second then said. "Just tell her your leader won't let you bring any samples anymore because you always eat them. Name a whole bunch of flavors and talk slowly."

Becky looked doubtfully at Amy Jo then at the house. It was hopeless. "All right," she said uncertainly.

Amy Jo nodded her head. "Good. I'll meet you back here when we're done," she said, then turned to make her way down the row of shrubs to the back of the house. As she reached the corner, she cast one last glance over her shoulder and saw Becky staring at her from the same spot she'd just left. Amy Jo slumped her shoulders for a second, then motioned frantically for Becky to move on up to the house.

Becky walked unsteadily towards the driveway and headed up to the front door. She raised her fist to knock, then lowered it and glanced longingly down the road where the ponies were tied. Becky closed her eyes, weighing which worried her more, Maggie, or Amy Jo if she failed to go through with the plan. In the end, she raised her fist and knocked on the door.

Becky released her breath slowly and was about to turn away when the door opened and a man stepped out. "Who are you?" he asked.

Becky's eyes traveled the length of his frame. His body was shadowed by the hall light behind him, creating dark, carved out hollows where his eyes should have been. His black hair was pulled straight back from his hatless head. The lower part of his face was deeply tanned, rendering his protected forehead even more pale by contrast. Jim. She swallowed hard.

Five hundred cotton balls stuffed in her mouth couldn't have made her tongue feel more dry. She opened her mouth, but nothing came out except some kind of garbled squeak.

Jim frowned as he loomed over her. "Well?" he asked.

Becky cleared her throat and did her best to swallow again. "I'm the, I mean, I'm a G-Girl Scout."

"I see," he said, slowly beginning to roll up his left shirt sleeve.

Becky's knees began to tremble as he rolled up the right one. "I'm selling c-cookies." The trembling in her knees had shifted to her throat.

Jim shook his head as he cracked his knuckles. "Mrs. Martin is sick and Maggie and I are not interested in buying Girl Scout cookies," he said as he checked over his shoulder.

Her ears were on pause. "We have ch-chocolate chip . . ." she began slowly, "and we also have ginger snaps and, uh, lemon d-drops and snicker doodles and . . ."

Jim drew his lips together in irritation. "So where are your boxes of cookies? If you really are a Girl Scout selling cookies, you should have brought them along," he said suspiciously.

Becky's eyebrows rose. "Boxes? Of cookies?" she asked, blinking her eyes. "Uh, my leader won't give me any because I always eat all of the cookies," she recited from memory.

Jim looked down at her with eyes half closed. "Eating the cookies without paying for them, is that it?" he said accusingly.

Becky's cheeks grew hot. "It's not like that. I'm not a thief!"

Steps could be heard from the hallway. "Come on, Jim, it's late; dinner's getting cold," came the sound of a woman's voice. "Get rid of whoever it is."

Jim gave her one last look. "Can't help you," he said before shutting the door.

Becky leaned against the post beside her and closed her eyes. The second time she pushed herself away from the post she found her legs could hold her up and she made her way down the driveway. At the corner, she saw Amy Jo wildly motioning for her to hurry.

"What's the matter?" asked Becky anxiously as she reached their meeting place.

Amy Jo took her friend's arm and guided her to a spot further down the row of shrubs. "The furniture has been moved around in one of the rooms on the first floor," she said as she hurried along. "Some of it's been pushed to the middle of the room and there're some boxes on top of the tables."

"Maybe they're helping her pack," suggested Becky. "Remember, she said she couldn't live here without help. They probably can't help her with the work around here any more, so she's moving out."

Amy Jo shook her head. "I don't think that's it," she said. "Mrs. Martin would have said something about moving when I saw her." Amy Jo shifted her weight and sighed as her eyes surveyed the back yard. "Do you see that tree right over there?" she asked, pointing to a tall tree with branches reaching above the second story.

Becky's eyes trailed up the height of the tree. "Tell me you're not thinking what I think you're thinking."

"Just tell me this," said Amy Jo, measuring the tree with her eyes. "What was Maggie doing just now when you left the house?"

"I talked to Jim."

Amy Jo turned back and looked at Becky. "Really? He was in the house, too? Hm. So, what were *they* doing?"

"Maggie was calling him in for dinner," answered Becky.

Amy Jo nodded her head. "So they'll be busy long enough for me to climb up to the second floor, crawl through the window, and put the marked money in Mrs. Martin's handbag."

Becky began to wring her hands. "What if you fall, or what if they come out, or what if Mrs. Martin's awake . . ."

"Look, I can climb trees with one hand tied behind my back," she assured her friend. "All you have to do is stand by and whistle if somebody comes out the back door. Anyway, she always gets a sleeping pill in the evening."

Becky looked longingly down the road again in the direction of the ponies. "Can we go home when you get back?"

"Sure," said Amy Jo as she parted the shrubs and stepped through. "I'll be back before you know it."

CHAPTER 8

Conspiracy

Foothold, Amy Jo thought as she scouted around the tree looking for a place to start her climb. She found a wedge formed by two branches, then placed her foot in the middle, grabbed the branch above the spot where her foot rested, and heaved herself up. Several minutes later and completely out of breath, she was waist high to the ledge of Mrs. Martin's window. Her old friend lay very still, her eyes closed.

Beads of sweat began to trickle down Amy Jo's face as she tried to lift up the window. *Don't have enough leverage,* she decided. *Have to get closer to the window.* She took two more careful steps and reached under the window again. This time the window gave and Amy Jo lifted until there was enough room for her to slip her leg over the windowsill. "Don't look down," she muttered to herself as she grabbed hold of the window frame and hauled herself inside the room.

Amy Jo quietly slid down to the floor and rested until her breath was under control. Her eyes nervously darted between Mrs. Martin's face and the doorknob leading into the bedroom. Slowly, she raised herself and tiptoed to the table where Mrs. Martin's handbag lay. After another quick peek at Mrs. Martin and the door, Amy Jo opened the handbag, took out the billfold, and reached in her pocket for the hundred dollars in marked ten dollar bills. Her hands shook as she slipped them quickly into the billfold and placed it back into the handbag, then eased the clasp soundlessly over the catch.

The window seemed a mile away as she took her first step away from the table. Out of nowhere, voices came from the stairway and were approaching the bedroom door fast. Amy Jo reached the window, placed her hand on the ledge, and looked down. *Suicide for sure if I try to hurry*, she decided, then dove behind the billowy drape and stilled it quickly with both hands.

"I'm sure I dropped my pen in Mrs. Martin's room," she heard Miss Windle say. "I'll only be a minute."

The door was opened quietly and Miss Windle stepped inside, noiselessly closing the door behind herself. She leaned against the door for a second, then tiptoed to the bed and leaned over her patient. She nodded her head as she watched the blankets rise and fall at regular intervals with Mrs. Martin's breathing, then straightened up and looked slowly around the room. Her eyes narrowed as she spied the tall, finely carved chest of drawers. She walked noiselessly across the carpet and eased open the top drawer. Her hands flew over the contents, patted them back into place, then moved onto the next drawer. Halfway down, a drawer squeaked. Miss Windle froze as she heard Mrs. Martin stir. Slowly, she turned her head and held her breath. Satisfied that her patient was still asleep, she continued her search.

From behind the drapes, Amy Jo watched in puzzled fascination as Miss Windle carefully searched under all the folded clothes.

When the last drawer had been closed, Miss Windle stood up, a crease forming between her eyes as she looked around the room, studying each piece of furniture carefully.

From the landing, Maggie's footsteps could be heard. Quickly, Miss Windle grabbed a pen from her purse and hurried to the door.

"Exactly where I thought it would be," she whispered as she met Maggie at the door. "Don't trouble yourself walking me to the front door. I can let myself out," she continued, then hurried down the stairs.

Maggie stood in the doorway chewing on her lower lip as she watched Mrs. Martin sleeping, then leaned back to check the stairway. Quietly, she closed the door and walked to the table where Mrs. Martin's handbag had been placed. Taking one last peek toward the sleeping woman, Maggie opened the handbag, dug out the billfold, and extracted a handful of ten dollar bills, then slipped them into her pocket. She crossed the room quickly and opened the door. The outline of a man was just visible from where Amy Jo stood. Maggie looked at him, and patted the pocket where she had placed the money. Jim looked into Maggie's eyes and nodded his head, then the door was closed and retreating footsteps could be heard on the stairs.

*   *   *   *

For several minutes, Amy Jo stayed behind the drapes, paralyzed by what she had witnessed. *It's a conspiracy. They're all a bunch of crooks*! she thought. *There's not one honest person in this whole house except for me and Mrs. Martin.* Amy Jo closed her eyes and leaned against the wall, then shot up straight. *I gotta get out of here!*

Amy Jo quickly slid her leg over the ledge, grabbed hold of the same limb, and swung onto the branch just below it. Holding on with one hand, she eased the window down and, limb by limb, made her way to the ground again.

Her legs felt about as secure as Silly Putty as she hurried back to the row of shrubs. "Let's go!" she said breathlessly, popping through the bushes.

Becky looked at her as they trotted down the road. "You don't look too good," she said.

"You wouldn't look too good either if you'd seen what I just saw," she answered.

"What happened?"

"Tell you later."

Oreo and Ginger neighed and shook their heads as they saw the girls approach.

Quickly placing a hand over their ponies' muzzles, the girls unknotted the lead ropes that had tied the ponies to the mailbox. They fastened bridles into place and stuffed the halters and lead ropes into their saddlebags.

The mare stepped forward as Amy Jo slipped her foot into the stirrup.

"Whoa, Ginger!" said Amy Jo sharply, then softened her voice. "Hold still, girl."

Becky stood at Oreo's head until she was sure the pony was ready to stand still, then quickly got into the saddle.

As soon as they were headed for home Becky turned to her friend. "Okay, so what happened?" she pressed again.

Amy Jo closed her eyes for a second then looked over at her friend. "It's just like I told you, Beck, they're all a bunch of crooks trying to get at her money."

Becky placed her fist on her leg. "But what happened?" she repeated.

Amy Jo let out her breath. "I got into Mrs. Martin's room okay and planted the money in her billfold. I was at the window ready to climb down the tree again when I heard the nurse in the hallway. She came back to the house looking for a pen." She looked at Becky as she said the last four words. "Huh! Was that a joke!"

"What do you mean?"

Amy Jo rolled her eyes. "Well, I didn't have time to get out the window, so I ducked behind a curtain and watched as she started going through Mrs. Martin's dresser. When she heard Maggie come walking up the steps, she whipped out a pen from her purse and said she'd found it."

"She didn't!"

"She did!" Amy Jo assured her. "Then, after Miss Windle left, Maggie checked the hallway to make sure she'd gone, came back and took the money I planted and put it in her pocket!"

"No!" Becky's eyes were twice their normal size. "You mean she has our feed money in her pocket!?"

"I'm telling you that's exactly where it is," announced Amy Jo.

Becky rode silently for a moment and let everything sink in. "What are we going to do now?" she asked.

Amy Jo sat back in her saddle and stared straight ahead. "We'll stake out the place after we deliver the papers tomorrow morning. There are some trees across the road from her house where we can hide," she said. "If Maggie or Jim leave to go to the village, we'll hop on our ponies and follow them. If one of them buys something with the marked money, we'll go to Officer Higgins at the police station."

"Police," Becky sighed. "Guess there's no other way?"

Amy Jo shook her head. "Nope, no other way."

CHAPTER 9

Diana's Dress Shop

Amy Jo parted the branches of a low hanging tree. "Did you bring anything to eat?" she asked, peering across the street at Mrs. Martin's driveway.

Becky sat up on the blanket. "Yeah," she said as she opened her saddlebag. "I figured we'd be here for a while, so I brought us both a peanut butter and jelly sandwich and something to drink."

Amy Jo took a bite, but kept her eyes on the driveway. "Thanks," she said.

The ponies stood head to tail swatting flies off each other's shoulders.

Becky laid back down and pulled her left arm up to her face. *Three o'clock*, she sighed looking at her watch. "How much longer do you think . . ."

Amy Jo leaned forward. "Did you hear that?!" she asked. "It's Jim's truck!"

Becky jumped up from the blanket, tightened Oreo's girth, and swung herself onto the saddle.

Amy Jo flipped the reins over Ginger's head. "Come on," she said, placing her foot in the stirrup. "Let's go."

They gave the truck time to get a head start, then parted the branches and slipped through. Keeping the ponies to the side of the road, the girls cantered the two blocks to the village then pulled up sharply and scanned the parking spots looking for the dusty truck.

"There it is," said Amy Jo, pointing to a spot in front of Diana's Dress Shop.

"What's Jim doing in a dress shop?" Becky wondered.

Amy Jo shrugged her shoulders. "He probably let Maggie borrow his truck," she suggested, then slipped down from her pony and handed the reins to Becky. "Just wait for me over there in the alley between Hank's Ice Cream Store and Double E and I'll be back in a jiffy," she said.

Becky looked up at the signs along the street. "I don't see anything that says Double E," she said.

Amy Jo closed her eyes and nodded her head. "Oh, yeah, I forgot, everyone around here calls it Double E, but it's really E.E. Hardware Store. You know, Double E means two E's."

Becky nodded her head. "Okay, I get it," she said.

Amy Jo crossed the street and edged up to the shop window. She cupped her eyes against the glass, scanning the interior of the store until she saw Maggie admiring herself in a three-way mirror. *Hm*, she thought to herself, *she looks different.*

Amy Jo waited until Maggie returned to the dressing room, then slipped quietly in the door and crawled under a circular dress rack close to the cash register.

Maggie smoothed down another dress as she returned to the mirror, then placed her hands on her hips, first turning to the left, then the right.  Next, she pivoted slowly around, tilting her head to see the back of the dress.

She's . . . pretty, Amy Jo thought with a touch of surprise.

Maggie faced the mirror and smoothed her hair back, then leaned forward pressing her lips inward to even out her lipstick. A smile played at the corners of her mouth. After brushing a fleck of mascara away from the corner of her eye, she turned abruptly and walked back to the dressing room.

Beads of sweat trickled down Amy Jo's face and she picked up the sleeve of a dress and began to fan herself. *Hm,* she thought pulling the dress inside the circular rack, *this is the kind of dress my mom would wear. Birthday's next month, too.*

Moments later Maggie came out wearing her old clothes with the new dress slung over her arm. She opened her purse as she stepped up to the counter.

Diana, the shop owner, folded the dress and brought out tissue paper and a pink-and-white-striped bag. "The dress looked great on you." She smiled as she rang up the amount on the cash register. "Thirty-six dollars, please," she said, pushing the receipt across the counter.

Maggie opened her purse and drew out her bill-fold.

Amy Jo's eyes widened as four ten dollar bills were slid across the counter. She reached up and inched the clothes in front of her aside, then leaned forward, her eyes glued to the counter. *Can't see!* She gritted her teeth and clenched her fist, her mind racing. Quickly, she placed her foot on the supporting bar and stretched up as tall as she could.

As Diana collected the money and placed it in the cash register, Amy Jo held her breath and shifted her weight forward. Suddenly, her foot slipped. She grabbed the bar holding the clothes and tried to steady everything, but lost her balance and pulled the entire circular rack over on top of herself. There was a terrible bang and clatter as the rack hit the floor. Amy Jo landed in a heap with dresses piled on top of her everywhere.

The sound of clicking high-heeled shoes walked around from behind the counter and stopped a few inches from her face. Layers of dresses were angrily tossed aside.

"Hi!" said Amy Jo brightly as she looked into Diana's angry golden eyes. "I suppose you're wondering what I'm doing here," she said, forcing a smile.

Diana tossed her golden hair aside and placed her hands on her slender hips. "This had better be good, Amy Jo," she said with an edge on her voice as she surveyed the rumpled dresses laying on the floor.

"Well," said Amy Jo, clearing her throat twice and crossing her legs, "I just happened to be outside and thought I'd run in here for a few minutes," she began slowly. "My mom's birthday is next month, you know—well, you probably don't know, but anyway I saw a dress in there that would look great on my mom. Of course, she hasn't tried it on yet, but at least I think—"

"All right, all right," sighed Diana, closing her eyes for a moment. "Never mind."

Maggie stared at Amy Jo. "Aren't you the paper girl?" she asked.

"Uh, actually, I used to deliver papers about a year ago, but then I quit." Amy Jo stalled as she scrambled to her feet. "But, uh, now I'm delivering papers again," she finally admitted.

Gathering courage, she stepped over the dresses on the floor, and up to the counter. "Nice," she said, nodding at the dress, while trying to peer into the cash register.

Maggie glanced at Amy Jo in surprise. "Thanks," she answered.

Diana slipped behind the counter, handed Maggie her four dollars in change, then gave the cash register drawer a shove. "How about cleaning up that mess?" she asked, folding Maggie's new dress and placing it in the bag.

Amy Jo's face fell as she looked at the closed cash register, then followed Diana's gaze to the heap of dresses on the floor. "Oh, sure," she said as she picked up the rack. "Sorry," she added.

Diana sighed and shook her head as she walked Maggie to the door. "I'm sorry about all this," she apologized as she held the door open. "Thank you for coming."

Several minutes later, Amy Jo walked across the street and joined Becky.

Ginger stepped forward and nudged Amy Jo's pocket. "Not now, girl," she said absently, stroking her pony's neck.

"How did it go?" asked Becky, looking curiously at her silent friend.

Amy Jo cleared her throat. "Not as well as I'd hoped," she answered vaguely.

Becky crossed her arms. "What's that suppose to mean?"

"Well," Amy Jo hedged, "let's just put it this way. The next time my mom goes to Diana's Dress Shop, I think I'd better stay home."

Becky opened her mouth to press for more answers, but decided to hold back.

Amy Jo drew the reins through her arm, stuffed her hands in her pockets, and leaned against the side of E.E. Hardware Store. "Now our paper route money is in Diana's cash register and we're not going to get it back unless we do something *drastic*," she said, staring across the street.

Becky looked up quickly. "In the cash register!?" *What happened to sticking to the suspect like glue*, she thought disgustedly. "How drastic?" she asked instead, quickly working Oreo's reins between her fingers.

Amy Jo stood up straight and grabbed Ginger's reins. "Let's put the ponies in Hank's paddock behind his store. I do it all the time. He doesn't mind," she said, heading down the alley.

Becky tugged at Oreo's reins, trying to catch up. "You didn't tell me what you meant by drastic," she said.

"We're going to have to go to the police station and talk to Officer Higgins," said Amy Jo as she untacked Ginger. "Somehow we've got to convince him that our

forty dollars is in Diana's cash register and
that Maggie stole Mrs. Martin's money."

CHAPTER 10

H.H. Higgins

Amy Jo stormed into the Bedford Police Station with her partner close behind. The sign on the desk said "H.H. Higgins."

Officer Higgins glanced up from his computer. "Hi, Amy Jo. How's my junior detective doing?" he asked, his stubby fingers pecking out keys on the keyboard.

Amy Jo let out a sigh as she came to a halt in front of his desk. "It's like this," she began in a rush. "Mrs. Martin hired Jim and Maggie to help her out after the Emersons left, right?"

Officer Higgins adjusted his glasses and studied the monitor. "Yep, that's what they tell me," he said as he deleted the last two letters from the screen.

"Then, she got sick and had to have this nurse, Miss Windle, stop by every day, right?"

"Yep, I heard that, too."

"Okay, now, there's absolutely no doubt that one of them is stealing money from her."

Officer Higgins stopped working at the computer and swiveled around in his chair to look at the girls. "Now wait a minute," he said, holding up his hands and leaning his broad frame back in his chair. "What makes you think one of them is stealing money from Mrs. Martin?"

Amy Jo shot a quick look at the door, then leaned forward and lowered her voice. "Last week when I stopped at her house to collect for the paper route, she reached in her handbag to pay me and a hundred dollars was missing." She studied him for a reaction. When none came, she added, "I mean she's really groggy, but she'd know if she was missing a hundred dollars!"

Officer Higgins nodded. "I heard that you'd bullied, I mean talked Mrs. Davis into letting you take over Jennie and Andi's paper routes for the summer," he sighed, running his fingers through his thin, dark hair. "Mrs. Martin had a stroke, you know, Amy Jo. Maybe she's confused and just forgot how much money she had." Officer Higgins glanced over at Becky. "This must be your new partner."

"Oh, yeah, sorry," said Amy Jo, remembering her manners. "Officer Higgins, this is Becky Allison," she said, making a quick introduction, then jumped right back to the subject. "I know she had a stroke, but I just think you ought to check Diana's cash register anyway because our money's in there."

Officer Higgins leaned his head back for a moment, his blue eyes studying the tiled ceiling. "Now you tell me . . . *why* . . . should I check Diana's cash register?" he asked, returning his gaze to Amy Jo.

Amy Jo placed her hands on her hips. "Because the marked money that we took from the paper route is in there," she explained.

Frustration and amusement battled for position on Officer Higgins' face. "Maybe you'd better start explaining a little earlier in the story," he said, folding his short, thickset arms.

"Okay," said Amy Jo, looking over his head and pressing her lips together. "I inked in the first and last zeros on ten dollar bills, then I climbed the tree beside Mrs. Martin's bedroom and put them in her handbag to set a trap for the person who stole her money," she began slowly. "The nurse came in and rummaged through her dresser and then Maggie came in and took the money out of Mrs. Martin's billfold."

Officer Higgins leaned forward curiously. "Where were you when all of this was happening?" he asked.

"Behind the curtain," she said quickly. "Then, this morning, Becky and I waited across the road and when Maggie left the house for Diana's Dress Shop, we followed her into the village. It's not that far, you know."

Officer Higgins nodded his head. "And what were you doing while Amy Jo was in Diana's shop?" he asked, looking at Becky.

"Uh." Becky's mind turned blank under the officer's stare and she blinked her eyes. "I held the ponies in the alley between the ice cream shop and E.E. Hardware," she finally answered.

"Then," Amy Jo jumped in, "I followed Maggie into the shop and hid inside one of the racks. But, the problem was I couldn't get close enough to check the markings on the money before Diana closed the cash register." Amy Jo leaned forward, placing her hands on his desk. "So that's why you need to go over and check her cash register."

Officer Higgins took his glasses off and slowly began to clean them. "I need more proof of guilt, Amy

Jo," he began. "Maggie works for Mrs. Martin and maybe she took the money to buy medicine or food or something for her. While she's in town, maybe she decided to do some shopping on her own."

"I know, but couldn't you take a peek inside Diana's cash register anyway?" pleaded Amy Jo. "She probably wouldn't mind."

Officer Higgins looked up. "I'm not going to upset innocent citizens without more to go on than this, Amy Jo," he said, firmly replacing his glasses. "I need more evidence to start an investigation."

"Oh-h, all right," said Amy Jo, stuffing her hands in her pockets. "We'll get more evidence."

"Now, don't go messing with something that's none of your business, Amy Jo," cautioned Officer Higgins.

Becky opened the door to leave but was pushed aside as a large, middle-aged woman came crashing through. The yellow plastic daisy bobbed up and down on her hat as she marched up to the officer's desk.

Officer Higgins took off his glasses again and pinched the bridge of his nose with his thumb and forefinger in a pained expression. "Afternoon, Mildred," he sighed.

"Good afternoon, yourself," she squeaked, then leaned forward so that her face was only a foot from his.

"Something very odd has been happening over at the house and I want you to do something about it," she demanded, pressing her lips firmly together.

The door closed behind the girls as they crossed the street and headed for the paddock to get their ponies.

Ginger and Oreo looked up and neighed as they saw the girls approaching.

Amy Jo reached in her pocket for two peppermint starbursts and gave one to Becky. Even ten feet away the ponies heard the crackle of the paper being unwrapped and began to nod their heads. "I know what we'll do," she said, holding out her hand to Ginger.

Oreo ate the candy out of Becky's hand and then nudged her arm for more. "That's all I have, you greedy pony," she said, then turned to her partner. "I'm listening."

Ginger shook her head while Amy Jo tried to slip the bit between her pony's teeth. "Hold still, Ginger," she said. "We'll ride back to Mrs. Martin's house while Maggie's still in the village," she began. "Then, we can search for the money box and go upstairs to see if all the money was taken out of Mrs. Martin's billfold."

Becky's mouth dropped open as they mounted their ponies and guided them through the gate. "What if Maggie comes back while we're still there?" she asked.

"That's why we've got to hurry," said Amy Jo, kicking Ginger into a canter.

CHAPTER 11

The Hiding Place

The doorknob turned easily and the girls slipped into the hallway. It was dim after the brightness of the sun and they stood motionless for a moment until their eyes adjusted.

Amy Jo pulled the side window curtain back slightly and peered outside. "I'd feel a lot better if I knew where Jim was," she whispered, licking her lips. She took a deep breath and turned around.

Becky stood eyeing the hallway nervously.

"Come on, Beck," said Amy Jo, leading the way. "I'll show you what I meant about them moving the furniture in the room at the back of the house."

It was a small room with a row of windows facing the back lawn. In the center of this row of windows was a door that opened to a patio. The furniture along the back wall across from the windows had been moved and in its place stood a bed with a small table beside it.

Becky curiously studied the arrangement, then turned to Amy Jo. "There's not much of a mystery here," she decided. "It looks to me like they've turned this into a bedroom."

Amy Jo faced the back of the room and stared at the bed. "That's what it looks like to me, too," she agreed. "But who's going to sleep here, that's what I'd like to know." Amy Jo stood still as she remembered what Mrs. Martin had said. *'The nurse has threatened to move in if I don't get better soon.'* Then moving to the door, she motioned for Becky to follow her out of the room.

They retraced their steps back to the hallway. Amy Jo stepped soundlessly up the stairs, but stopped as she heard Becky trip on the second step, the same place she'd tripped on her last visit. She frowned as she turned to tell her friend to be more careful, then stopped dead and stared at the space where the carpet had been edged back.

Amy Jo steadied herself with the banister as she made her way quickly down the stairs. The girls inspected the recessed handle partly hidden by the carpet. Becky held the carpet back allowing Amy Jo to open the secret door. Inside, lay a long, narrow, metal box.

As they eased the box out of the hiding place, the front door creaked open behind them. Amy Jo and Becky swung around, the color draining from their faces.

"I see you've found the old lady's money," said Miss Windle. The light was behind her, casting her face in a shadow.

She walked slowly toward the stairs. "I never thought to look there," she continued, her voice cool and menacing. "It was very clever of you to find it for me."

Becky froze where she was. Amy Jo placed a protective hand on the money box.

"I'd planned to move into the back room so I could spend more time searching." She'd almost reached the bottom of the steps. "But now, it appears I won't have to."

Amy Jo stole a glance at Becky as if to say, I knew that's what she planned to do.

Miss Windle stared at Amy Jo with one eye and Becky with the other one. "Now, you two be good little girls and step back," she said, a glint shining from her eyes. "If you stay out of the way, you won't get hurt."

Amy Jo wrapped her fingers around the handle and drew it with both hands to her chest.

"Don't get any stupid ideas about taking off with that box," warned Miss Windle, her voice raising several pitches. "I've worked hard looking for that money and it's mine." She reached over and wrestled the box away from Amy Jo's grasp.

Amy Jo wet her lips. "You're not going to get away with this," she said as threateningly as she could.

Miss Windle gave a sharp laugh. "And why not?" she asked, tucking the box under her arm.

"Because . . ." Amy Jo's mind raced furiously, "because as soon as you leave I'll call the police!"

Miss Windle's eyes narrowed as she laid the box down and drew closer to the girls. "Have you ever seen Mrs. Martin's basement?" she asked in a hushed voice. "There are spiders and rats down there," she continued slowly.

The girls widened their eyes and flattened themselves against the wall. "How about if we agree to leave quietly and keep our mouths shut?" asked Amy Jo in a sudden change of heart.

"It's very dark down there, too." Miss Windle stepped closer, reaching out with her claw-like hands. "It has a lock on the door and there is only one way out."

Amy Jo stole another quick glance at her friend. "We won't tell a soul. Cross our hearts and hope to die, right, Beck?"

Becky gave her a frantic look.

"Well," said Amy Jo, having second thoughts. "Forget about the hope to die part."

Becky nodded her head vigorously, turning saucer-sized eyes back to Miss Windle.

With the speed of a lizard's tongue, Miss Windle darted out and grabbed the girls around their forearms. The girls struggled to free themselves, but her hands felt like two giant clamps.

Amy Jo tried to kick her in the shins, but Miss Windle saw it coming and sidestepped. The basement door was under the staircase and it took Miss Windle only seconds to drag them there. She shoved Becky up against the wall and pinned her with her side while she opened the door and threw Amy Jo onto the landing of the first step. Then, she grabbed Becky and threw her beside Amy Jo. The last thing the girls saw was Miss Windle ripping off her nurse's cap before the door was slammed shut and the key turned.

After Miss Windle left, the house sounded deathly quiet except for the thundering noise coming from each girl's chest.

"There's got to be a light switch around here somewhere," said Amy Jo nervously as her hands searched the wall beside the doorway. "Get up here and help me look, Becky."

"I don't know if I can s-stand up," said Becky shakily. "Anyway, after we get out of here, I'm going to resign as Dr. Watson," she sniffed.

"I don't blame you," said Amy Jo apologetically. "But don't wimp out yet. We've got to stop that old witch before she gets away with Mrs. Martin's money!"

Becky wiped her nose with the back of her hand and got to her feet. She began to feel the wall opposite Amy Jo. "Here it is," she said, flipping on the switch.

The girls blinked their eyes and looked around. They studied the narrow ledge of the landing on the first step leading down to the basement.

"Good thing she didn't push any harder," worried Amy Jo, looking down to the bottom of the stairs.

Becky swallowed hard and nodded her head as her eyes searched the corners for signs of rats or spiders.

Amy Jo closed one eye and looked through the keyhole. "Good news," she reported. "I can't see anything."

Becky looked over at her friend in surprise. "How can that be good news?"

"It means the key is still in the lock."

Becky shook her head. "Doesn't do us any good unless one of us is skinny enough to slide under the door."

Amy Jo gave her friend a sidelong glance before heading down the stairs. "You don't watch many detective shows do you?" she called over her shoulder.

Becky scrambled down to catch up. "What are you doing?" she asked as she watched her friend open up two sheets of newspaper she'd taken from a stack in the corner, then line them up side by side on the floor.

"Just watch," said Amy Jo as she began to tear off strips of masking tape to bind the two pieces of news-paper together. She searched the peg board on the wall until she found a slender screw driver, then yanked it off its hook, grabbed the newspapers and marched up the stairs, a bewildered Becky clambering behind her.

Amy Jo squatted down in front of the doorknob, slipped the newspaper under the door, then took the screwdriver and wiggled it through the lock in the door until she made contact with the tip of the key. She gave a quick jab which knocked the key onto the newspaper on the other side of the door. Carefully, Amy Jo pulled the newspaper back under the door until the key appeared.

Becky watched in admiration as Amy Jo leaned over and picked it up.

Amy Jo grinned as she held it up to show her friend. "See," she said, "it's one of those long, black skeleton keys. It pops right out if you jab it from either side."

Amy Jo inserted the key into the lock, and shoved the door open. She reached around, grabbed Becky by the arm, and pulled her into the hallway.  Halfway to the door, they jerked to a halt. In the doorway stood Miss Windle, her claws reaching out to grab them again.

CHAPTER 12

Stand Back or I'll Shoot

Becky screamed as Miss Windle advanced from the doorway. Amy Jo held the slender screwdriver out in front of her. "Stand back or I'll shoot!" she screamed.

A surprised Officer Higgins stuck his head around the door, then shoved his cap on the back of his head. "Your gun is missing a few parts, wouldn't you say, Amy Jo?" he said, scratching behind his ear with one hand as he laid the money box on the table with the other.

The girls slumped against the wall, the screwdriver slipping out of Amy Jo's hand.

"How did you know to come here?" asked Amy Jo, her head leaning against the wall.

Officer Higgins took out his handcuffs and clamped one end around Miss Windle's wrist and attached the other end to the banister. "There was a woman who came in after you left the police station," he said over his shoulder. "She suspected that the nurse taking care of her mother was stealing from her," he continued as he turned around to face them. "That was just too much of a coincidence in my book."

Amy Jo gave a disgusted sigh. "There's more than that," she began, nodding her head toward the scowling woman. "Miss Windle was planning to move in so she could search the house for Mrs. Martin's money box!"

"You'll never be able to prove that!" screeched the handcuffed woman. "It's just your word against mine," she spat, glaring at the girls. Then she turned to the police officer. "When I walked through the door, I caught these two girls lifting the money box out of its hiding place," she said as she waved her free arm in the girls' direction. "I locked them in the basement until I could call the authorities!"

Officer Higgins looked at the woman disgustedly and shook his head, then turned his attention back to the girls. "There was something else. I remembered that you said Mrs. Martin seemed groggy. This woman's mother was groggy, too," he continued, giving the girls a knowing look. "The nurse was giving her mother too much medication to keep her sleepy so she wouldn't be suspicious that her money was disappearing."

Amy Jo stared at Officer Higgins for a few seconds, then nodded her head slowly. "Then, Miss Windle put it in everybody's head that Mrs. Martin was confused because of the stroke."

Just then, Maggie and Jim came bursting through the door.

Jim looked at the nurse handcuffed to the banister and turned to Officer Higgins. "I saw the police car outside. What's going on here?" he demanded.

Officer Higgins eyed Maggie and Jim. "It seems Miss Windle has been helping herself to some of her so-called patient's money."

Maggie looked up in surprise. "Why do you say 'so-called patient'?" she asked.

Officer Higgins shifted his weight and placed his hands on his hips. "Because I called the agency and got a description of the nurse they were supposed to send to

take care of Mrs. Martin and it doesn't match
Miss Windle," he answered. His eyes narrowed
as he studied the woman handcuffed to the
banister. "Who are you anyway?" he asked.

Miss Windle lifted her chin and turned her head
to the side.

Amy Jo straightened her shoulders. "You better tell
us or we'll throw you in the basement and lock the door!"
she said heatedly. "And I'll tell you something else, you
were right about the spiders and rats down there!"

A smirk appeared on Miss Windle's face as she
looked at Officer Higgins.

He studied her for a moment then held out his hand
to the girls. "Where's the key to the basement?" he asked
without taking his eyes off Miss Windle.

The smirk slowly left her face as she watched Amy
Jo lean over and pick up the key from the floor. "You
wouldn't!" she squeaked at the police officer.

"Watch me," he said softly.

"All right, all right," she said irritably. "I was
house sitting for the nurse from the agency and took the
two calls when they came in," she admitted, then lowered her eyes. "I'm a little short of cash right now and
figured I'd just borrow a little bit until my luck got better."

Maggie stepped forward. "You pretended to be a
nurse and gave medication to people," she said accusingly.

Miss Windle shrugged her shoulders. "I used to
be a nurse a long time ago," she said defensively. "I knew
what to do."

Becky looked up and frowned. "But these people
were old and you took money that didn't belong to you,"
she said steadily.

Jim gazed at Becky for a moment. "Weren't you selling Girl Scout cookies the other night?" he asked.

Becky felt her face grow warm under his scrutiny. "I was keeping you busy at the front door while Amy Jo searched the back of the house."

Maggie looked at Amy Jo in surprise. "Why did you want to search the house?" she asked.

"We thought you or Jim might be stealing money from Mrs. Martin," explained Amy Jo.

Maggie and Jim looked at each other, then returned their gaze to Amy Jo. "We thought *you* were the one stealing from Mrs. Martin," said Jim.

Amy Jo looked back in astonishment. "Me?! Why me?"

"Mrs. Martin complained of her money missing the same day you tried to collect for the newspaper," said Maggie. "When she opened up her handbag to pay you, the money was gone."

Jim nodded his head. "We figured that you'd managed to take out the money quickly while you were getting her purse at the table."

Amy Jo's mouth dropped open as she looked over at Becky. Then, she placed her hands on her hips and turned back to Maggie and Jim. "Yeah, but I put marked money in Mrs. Martin's purse and I saw *you* take it out the night Miss Windle came back looking for her pen," she said accusingly.

For a moment, Jim and Maggie stared at Amy Jo. "Where were you that you saw me take money out of Mrs. Martin's purse?" asked Maggie.

Amy Jo lifted her chin. "I climbed the tree outside the bedroom window and put marked money in Mrs. Martin's purse to try to catch whoever was stealing from her," Amy Jo explained. "Then I heard Miss Windle coming and hid behind the curtain.

Jim thought for a moment and then nodded his head. "Things are starting to fall into place now," he said.

Officer Higgins cleared his throat. "Would you mind including me in on this discussion," he asked, adjusting his cap on his head. "What things are falling into place?"

Jim shook his head as if he were trying to put all the pieces together. "Let me start from the beginning," he said, pressing his lips together while he collected his thoughts. "The day Amy Jo came to collect, Mrs. Martin was upset because money was missing from her purse. Both Miss Windle and Amy Jo had been in Mrs. Martin's room that morning and we weren't sure which one was the thief." He raised his eyebrows and leaned his head forward as he looked at Officer Higgins.

Maggie gave Jim a shy smile as she continued. "Jim hadn't been in the best of moods, but I went to him anyway and asked for advice."

Jim rolled his eyes. "I'll say I was in a bad mood. My girl back home had just written me a letter and dumped me. I could have hammered a thousand nails in every building on the property," he said with a grimace.

"I'll agree to that!" interrupted Amy Jo, then turned a deep shade of red when all eyes focused on her in surprise. "Uh, what I mean is . . . oh, never mind," she said, lowering her head.

Maggie stared at Amy Jo for another second then shrugged her shoulders. "We decided to set a trap the next time Miss Windle came to the house. Jim and I pooled our money together and put it in Mrs. Martin's billfold."

A light went on in Amy Jo's brain and she pressed the palm of her hand to her forehead and closed her eyes tightly. She looked over at Becky. "Can you believe that?" she asked, turning to Becky.

Becky screwed up her face. "Believe what?"

Amy Jo sighed loudly. "Jim and Maggie set a trap because they suspected us and we set a trap because we suspected them."

"Well, that's about it really," indicated Maggie. "Except that after Miss Windle left that night, I slipped into her room and the money I thought I'd placed there earlier hadn't been taken so I took it out and figured Miss Windle was innocent."

Officer Higgins' eyes narrowed. "So, when you thought Amy Jo was guilty, why didn't you report it to me?"

Jim looked at the floor a moment before answering. "She seemed like a nice enough kid, a little snoopy and pushy maybe, but we were hoping that Mrs. Martin's stroke had made her thinking fuzzy and that she was mistaken about the missing money. Anyway, we decided to keep a better watch on things when Amy Jo came to collect next time."

At the words snoopy and pushy, Becky covered her mouth and turned her head the other way, but not before a hint of a giggle escaped her lips.

Amy Jo looked over and placed her hands on her hips. "I heard that, Watson," she said heatedly.

Officer Higgins rubbed his hand over his mouth while he stepped over to Miss Windle. "Okay," he said in a muffled voice. "You'll have to come along with me." He unlocked the handcuff to the banister and attached it to her other arm. As Officer Higgins reached the doorway, he turned around. "I'll need for all of you to come down to the police station tomorrow and give a statement." He turned to the girls. "We'll see that you get your money back tomorrow when you come in." Then, he was gone.

The remaining four people stood look-  ing at the floor. Jim scratched his head while Maggie smoothed her hair down with her hand.

Amy Jo looked at Maggie for a moment. "You're not squinting anymore. I noticed it at Diana's Dress Shop."

"I'd lost my contacts and had to order another pair," she explained. "They just came in yesterday."

Amy Jo remembered how Maggie had looked at the shop. "So, did you show Jim your new dress?" she asked.

Becky reached over and poked Amy Jo with her elbow.

Amy Jo shot her a glance and mouthed the word "What!?"

Becky rolled her eyes then nodded her head towards the door.

Maggie looked nervously at her watch. "I'd better take some dinner up to Mrs. Martin," she said, smoothing her hair down again as she headed for the kitchen.

Jim was still scratching his head as he glanced at the two girls. "I'll help you," he said quickly, following Maggie into the kitchen.

Amy Jo's eyes fell on the money box Officer Higgins had placed on the table next to the door. "Let's take this upstairs and give it to Mrs. Martin," she said, picking it up and heading for the stairway.

"It'll cheer her up, that's for sure," said Becky, following her to the bedroom door.

They tapped quietly on the door and entered when they heard a faint "Come in."

"Hi, Mrs. Martin," said Becky, crossing to the side of the bed.

Amy Jo had placed the money box behind her back. "Guess what we found?" she asked, her eyes shining.

Mrs. Martin's face brightened up. "Did you find . . . ?"

The girls laughed as Amy Jo brought the box from behind her back and placed it on the edge of the bed.

Mrs. Martin covered her mouth with both hands. She held out her arms to both girls kissing first one then the other before clasping the box to her chest. "Thank you," she whispered softly then laid her head back on the pillow and closed her eyes.

"Maybe we'd better leave," suggested Becky quietly.

Amy Jo nodded her head and made her way down the stairs to the front door.

The girls were silent as they rode Ginger and Oreo down the lane towards the barn.

Becky turned in her saddle and looked at Amy Jo. "I'm glad we helped get Mrs. Martin's money back, but I'm glad it's over."

Amy Jo studied Becky for a moment. "Does this mean you're not going to quit being Dr. Watson?" she asked hopefully.

Becky shifted in her saddle and stared straight ahead, but answered evenly. "I'll still be your Dr. Watson," she said, then smiled at Amy Jo.

Amy Jo nodded her head. "Great, because there's been something odd going on down at the—"

"Oh, no, not yet!" cried Becky as she dug her heels into Oreo's side and cantered away.

"Maybe I'd better give her a couple of days between cases," muttered Amy Jo as she settled into her saddle.